Calamity Kite
and the Wayward Wind

Story by
ANITA POWELL
Illustration concepts by Janet Ray Breidenbaugh

ISBN 978-1-63885-087-8 (Paperback)
ISBN 978-1-63885-089-2 (Hardcover)
ISBN 978-1-63885-088-5 (Digital)

Covenant Books
11661 Hwy 707
Murrells Inlet, SC 29576
www.covenantbooks.com

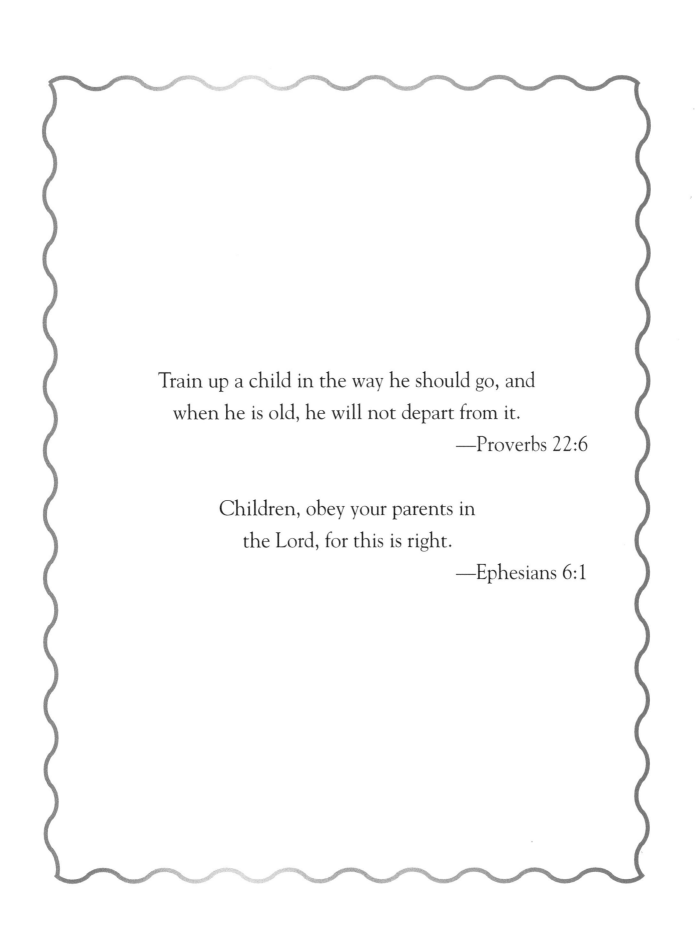

Train up a child in the way he should go, and
when he is old, he will not depart from it.

— Proverbs 22:6

Children, obey your parents in
the Lord, for this is right.

— Ephesians 6:1

"I wish I had a kite! I wish I had a kite! Oh, how I wish I had a kite!" sang Katie, as she skipped home from school. It was spring, and she felt happy.

Finding her mother, Mrs. Merryweather, in the kitchen, she exclaimed, "Mother! There is going to be a big kite-flying day at school. I need a kite!"

Mother said "Hmmm" and "I see" as Katie told her all about the prizes. There would be shiny yellow ribbons for the smallest kite and for the biggest kite. There would be rosy red ribbons for the scariest kite and for the funniest kite. There would be bright-blue ribbons for the kite that flew the highest and for the kite that stayed up the longest. All the other kites would get grass-green ribbons for flying on Kite Day.

"The rule is," she finished, "all kites have to be made at home."

Mrs. Merryweather looked thoughtful. *How do people make kites?* she wondered. *Maybe Daddy or Uncle Floyd would be able to help Katie build a good one.*

When Mr. Merryweather came home, he found Katie looking in a big book marked "K."

"I am looking up kites in the encyclopedia," she explained.

THE
WORLD BOOK
ENCYCLOPEDIA

K

4

After she told him all about Kite Day, he became excited about Kite Day too! "Let's go to the computer and look online for more ideas, instructions, and drawings," he suggested.

Mr. Merryweather and Katie looked at all kinds of kites before they decided which kite they would build.

Katie took the coins from her piggy bank and counted the coins from her purse. She was able to buy string and paper with her own money. Mr. Merryweather found the right kind of wood. Uncle Floyd picked up his tools and came to help. Together, they built a fine and fancy kite. The kite was also stout enough to last if a strong wind came up.

"Do you need any help learning to fly it?" asked Daddy.

Katie didn't think so. Out the door she ran with the kite.

"Up, kite, up!" she called as she ran. "And don't go near the bushes!"

Up flew the kite. Down he looked at Katie. He looked at the bushes.

I am a strong kite, he thought, *and Katie is not a very big girl. I don't need her to hold me back and guide me with that string. I can stay out of bushes without her help.*

The wind whispered to the kite, "Pull away! I will take you for a nice ride! Pull away!"

With some help from the wind, the kite gave a big yank on the string. The string got away from Katie!

"Come back!" she cried, "Look out!"

The wind was watching. The wind had been waiting. "Now," said the wind to the kite, "here is a nice ride for you!"

Up and around went the kite. *Oh, this is fun*, he thought. *No girl, no string…I like this much better!*

"Let's see how close we can fly to the bushes," the wind said, laughing.

"I am not supposed to go near the bushes," warned the kite.

Down and around went the kite. How exciting! Just then, the wind shoved him into the bushes! Pointed pieces were poking him all over. He could not get loose. *Where was the wind? Why didn't the wind blow and get him out?*

The wind had run away, laughing.

"Oh, you naughty kite!" scolded Katie as she came to untangle and rescue him from the bushes. "This is a calamity! *You* are a *calamity* kite!"

Calamity Kite was all scratched up. He also had a hole in his face. Katie had to tape it up before he could fly again. Calamity Kite was glad to be out of the bushes. He felt a nice little breeze blowing. He wanted to fly again. Katie decided it would be better to find a place without bushes for kite flying.

"Do you need any help?" asked Daddy.

Katie didn't think so. Out the door she ran with the kite.

"Up, kite, up!" she called as she ran. "But please stay away from electric wires!"

Up flew Calamity Kite. The wind began to whisper, "You don't need to be guided by that string. You are big enough to stay out of wires, aren't you? Let's take a nice ride!"

"You tricked me last time!" complained Calamity Kite.

"Oh, that was just a little accident," encouraged the wind, and he blew a little stronger.

It was exciting! Calamity Kite gave a pull on the string, and *whoosh*, he went sailing away!

"Oh no! He got away again!" cried Katie. "Be careful, Calamity Kite, be careful!"

"Let's see how close we can get to the wires without getting caught!" the wind said as it laughed.

Calamity Kite was worried. He did not quite trust the wind. Up on this side. Down on that side. Around and around. Calamity Kite did not get caught…not at first.

Then, the wind sent a twister. The twister caught Calamity Kite's tail. Around and around the wire it went. Calamity Kite could not get away! He looked around for the wind to help him, but the wind was gone.

There he hung, upside-down, by his tail. There he stayed all night in the rain. No one noticed him.

The next day, the wind came back. "Oh, my! I see you are in big trouble," he sneered.

"You got me up here. You should get me down!" exclaimed Calamity Kite.

"Okay, I will do something!" *Swoosh! Swoosh!* He blew the dizzy, dangling kite. *Swoosh! Swoosh!* The wind was having a good time blowing Calamity Kite back and forth!

Now, hanging by one's tail and being blown about is most uncomfortable! Calamity Kite felt terrible!

"Oh, me. Oh, my! If I ever get down from here, I will be good from now on and obey."

Just then, the wind came up with a blustering gust, and Calamity Kite heard something rip! Down he fell and landed headfirst in a pile of rocks! He couldn't move. He couldn't do anything, but look up at the wires. There he saw a long piece of his beautiful tail. It was still wound up in the wires. All he had left was a short, silly-looking piece of tail. How embarrassing!

There he lay all day, waiting for Katie or someone to find him. He felt very sorry for himself.

"Oh, you naughty kite," scolded Katie, when she finally found him, "You naughty Calamity Kite! Here, let me see how bad your scratches are…Well, you have another hole, but I think we can fix it. You will probably still be able to fly. I will patch you up again."

Calamity Kite was glad Katie found him and taped his tears. He was glad to be off that wire. He felt so good that he wanted to fly again.

"Katie, do you need any help?" asked Daddy.

Katie didn't think so. Out the door she ran with the kite.

"Up, kite, up!" she called as she ran. "But this time, try to stay out of trouble."

Higher and higher sailed Calamity Kite. Flying high was wonderful!

Just then, he heard the wind whispering, "You can only go as high as the string lets you, you know. That is never high enough! I can take you *much* higher!"

"You tricked me the first time. You tricked me, last time. I am afraid you will trick me again!" complained Calamity Kite. "I want to stay out of trouble."

"Oh, a little twister just got hold of your tail, but I got you down, didn't I?" answered the wind. "You are okay now. Let's fly high!"

So with a big tug on the string, Calamity Kite pulled away from Katie. He did go higher—much, much higher. Then he wondered, *How can I get down safely without Katie guiding me with the string?*

Soon he found out how he was going to get down. The wind grew tired of playing with the kite. The wind went away and dropped him. Katie saw Calamity Kite falling. Before she could reach him, he had landed in a mud puddle. What a mess he was!

"Oh, you poor, naughty kite," she said sadly. "What am I going to do with you?"

Calamity Kite could see that Katie was very upset and discouraged. What if she threw him away? What if she made a new kite that would listen and obey?

Instead she carefully lifted him out of the muddy puddle. Carefully, she wiped off the mud. Calamity Kite could see he had caused her a lot of trouble.

Mrs. Merryweather helped Katie give Calamity Kite a bath. Katie told her mother the problems she was having.

"Daddy and Uncle Floyd helped me make this nice kite," she explained. "I am trying to teach him to fly, but he does not obey. Then he gets into all kinds of trouble. He has lost a big piece of his tail. I have patched up two holes. Now he has gotten wet and muddy. If I can't trust him to fly right, I can't let him fly with the other kites on Kite Day at school."

"I understand how you feel," answered Mrs. Merryweather. "Sometimes, my little kite doesn't fly right either. Have you asked your daddy to help you? My heavenly Father helps me with my little kite."

Katie did not know Mother had a kite. "What do you mean, Mother? I never see you flying a kite."

"In a way, I was pretending about the kite." Her mother laughed. "*You* are my little *kite*. You see, God made you. Now I must teach you the right and safe things to do. When you disobey, you sometimes have problems, just like Calamity Kite. I ask God to help me guide you in the right direction. Why don't you ask your daddy to help you with your kite? He would like to help you, if you will be patient and listen."

By this time, Calamity Kite had been hung out to dry. He had heard Mrs. Merryweather giving Katie advice. He thought about what she said while he was getting dry.

This clothesline is for the birds! he thought miserably. *If I had obeyed, I could be flying instead of dripping.*

He knew that if he had listened and obeyed, he would still have a beautiful long tail. His face would not be scratched up either.

It pays to obey, he thought. *I will listen to directions. I do not want to ruin myself. From now on, I will be a Careful Kite, not a Calamity Kite. Katie will be surprised!*

When Mr. Merryweather came home, Katie took him out to look at Calamity Kite. She showed him the holes. She showed him the tail. She showed him where the mud had been.

"Can we save this kite, Daddy?" she asked. "I really do love him."

"He can still straighten up and fly right, I believe," Daddy answered.

Together, they talked about what to do. He gave Katie some good ideas on how to fly a kite and guide it with the string. He said that if Calamity Kite learned to fly right, he would put a nice long handsome tail on him for Kite Day. How happy Calamity Kite was to hear that! It was so embarrassing to have a tiny tail.

As Katie took the clothespins off, she explained to him, "Calamity Kite, this is your *last* chance. If you don't listen to directions and obey, you may *ruin* yourself. If you don't learn to fly right, we will have to sit and watch the other kites have all the fun on Kite Day."

This time, when Calamity Kite went up to fly, he did not listen to the wind whispering this and that. He was glad to know Katie was holding on tightly to the long string. Calamity Kite was being a careful kite. He was able to go so high that he was out of sight. Katie knew he was okay, because she could feel the tug on the string.

"Come on, now, Calamity," coaxed the wind. "Let's get rid of the string and race over the hill!"

"Oh no! I have caught on to your old tricks, Mr. Wind," answered Careful Kite, "You will have to find a careless kite to trick, now. I am no longer a calamity kite. I am a careful kite!" Katie wound the string around her stick and brought him safely down.

At last, it was Kite Day. There was a lot of excitement at school. The principal closed the school early. The boys and girls got their kites ready to fly. Colorful kites soon filled the air.

There were some very tiny kites. Careful Kite was not the smallest. There were giant kites. He was not the biggest. There were some very scary-looking kites and some very, very funny ones. Careful Kite was not scary nor funny. Who would stay up longest? Who would fly the highest?

The wind was there having a good time too. Some kites got away from their boys and girls. They flew over the hill. Some landed on the other side of town and were never seen again. Others got caught in bushes and wires.

Lots of kites got their strings and tails tangled and finally fell. Only a few kites flew very, very high.

It was such a lot of fun flying with all those different kinds of kites! It was a wonderful day! Calamity Kite was now Careful Kite. He had learned to fly right and flew very high!

He and Katie wondered if they would receive a ribbon. They were having a great time, even if they didn't happen to win one of the *special* ribbons…

…but I think they won a ribbon, don't you?

The End

Calamity Kite and the Wayward Wind

Theme: It pays to obey.

Scripture:

> Children, obey your parents in the Lord: for this is right. (Ephesians 6:1)
>
> Train up a child in the way he should go: and when he is old he will not depart from it. (Proverbs 22:6)

Emphasis:

> Obedience is rewarded. Disobedience brings trouble.
>
> We are responsible for our own actions. A person can *ruin* himself by being disobedient and doing wrong things.
>
> Positive family interaction is demonstrated.
>
> Children need their parents' help. God's children need His help.
>
> Trustworthiness is emphasized.

Topics for discussion:

How were the kite and Katie alike?

Unwillingness to accept help and instruction makes life harder.

Calamity Kite and Katie had to learn the hard way.

Avoid listening to the wrong voice.

Making excuses for wrong actions doesn't make them right.

A person can ruin himself and hurt others in the process.

If you are trustworthy in small things, more can be entrusted to you.

It is not necessary to win in order to enjoy an activity.

Calamity Kite was successful by simply learning to *fly right*—listen and obey.

About the Author

Anita Powell, native of Indiana and transplant to Escondido, California, has a love of children and the value of early childhood learning. Her bachelor's degree in secondary education was earned at Anderson University and master's degree in elementary education at St. Francis University, both of Indiana. At AU, she met and married her late husband, David Joe Powell, and together, they had two sons, Douglas and Tyler.

At SFU, she got her first real glimpse into the often overlooked and untapped learning potential of the very young, through Suzuki violin techniques. Although Mrs. Powell taught high school, it was later teaching primary grades that ignited her interest in children's literature. In reading a variety of children's books to her pupils, she saw how the stories stirred imagination and could help develop character.

With the insight gained in teaching young children and rearing her own sons, Mrs. Powell was inspired to write character-building stories for other parents who are looking for similar ways to reinforce values of the home and bring enrichment to their small children.

CPSIA information can be obtained
at www.ICGtesting.com
Printed in the USA
BVHW021003240322
632251BV00001B/1

9 781638 850878